Caribou Song

atíhko níkamon

Caribou Song

By **Tomson Highway**
Illustrations by **Brian Deines**

atihko nikamon

Tomson Highway ohci
osisopéhikéwina **Brian Deines**

HarperCollins*Publishers*Ltd

Joe and Cody lived with their mama, their papa, and Cody's black dog, Ootsie. They lived too far north for most trees. Most of the year the lakes and islands and rivers and hills were covered in snow.

Joe ékwa Cody kí-wícáyáméwak mána omámáwáwa ékwa opápáwáwa ékwa Cody océmisisa Otisiy. wáhyaw kíwéti-nohk ká-kí-wíkicik ita kékác ká-paskwahk. osám piko mána kapé-ayi sákahikanihk ékwa mistikohk ékwa sípihk ékwa wacihk mistahi mana kóna kí-apiw.

kapé-pipon mána atihkwa kí-pimitisahwéwak ayinánéw atimwak ékwa otápánákwa
é-kí-ápacihácik.

"mush!" ká-ta-tépwét mána pápá, ékwa aspin mána atimwak
é-sipwépahtácik.

"cha!" ká-ta-tépwét mána pápá ékwa atimwak óté isi mána ispahtáwak.

ekwa kíspin "u!" tépwéci, óté isi mína máná ispahtáwak.

All year long, they followed the caribou with a sled pulled by eight huskies.

"Mush!" Papa would yell, and the dogs would run straight forward.

"Cha!" he would shout, and they would turn right.

And when he yelled "U!" they turned left.

Joe played the accordion, the kitoochigan. From morning to night he played and sang, "Ateek, ateek! Astum, astum! Yo-ah, ho-ho! Caribou, caribou! Come, come! Yo-ah, ho-ho!"

kwayask mána ká-kitócikéw mána Joe okitócikana. ékwa ani kapé-kísik mána kitócikéw ékwa nikamo, "atihk, atihk! ástam, ástam! yó ah hó hó."

And from morning to night Cody danced.
He danced on the rocks, he danced on the ice,
he even danced under the full silver moon.

ékwa wísta Cody kapé-kísik mána nímihitow. asinihk
mána nímihitow, miskwamihk mána nímihitow ahpo
atámihk písim mána nímihitow.

péyakwáw ésa óma mína é-síkwaniyik ká-picihcik ministikohk. é-kí-kísi-mówácik atihkamikwa ékwa pahkwésikana, Joe ékwa Cody ká-nitawi-papámohtécik nócim-ihk ékwa namóya wahyaw ékota táwáyihk ká-sákapit mistasiniy.

"Cody," Joe ká-itwét, "óta máwaci miywásin. nikamotán ékwa nímihitotán atihkwak ohci. nímihito kiya otéskanak tápiskóc kispitona ka-isi-miciminaman ékwa niya nika-nikamon, 'atihk, atihk' nika-kitócikán. ékwa sémák mihcét atihkwak ta-takopahtáwak."

One day, at the end of May, the family stopped on an island. After a lunch
of whitefish and bannock, Joe and Cody wandered off and found a meadow
surrounded by forest. In the middle stood a great big rock.

"Cody," said Joe. "This is the perfect spot. Let's sing and dance for the caribou.
You dance with your arms up like antlers. I'll sing 'Ateek, ateek' and play kitoochigan.
And before you know it, ten thousand caribou will burst out of the forest."

So Cody raised his arms to look like antlers, and began to dance. He lifted his left moccasin, then his right. Then his left, and then, *oof!* There he was, flat on a tuft of pillow-soft caribou moss poking through the melting snow.

ékwáni Cody ohpinam otéskana ékwa sipwé-nímihitow. ohpinam péyak osit níkán, ékota ohci kotak. ékota ohci kotak, ékota ohci, *oof!* ékota ká-cípatapit ita askiy apisís ká-nókwasik kónihk ohci.

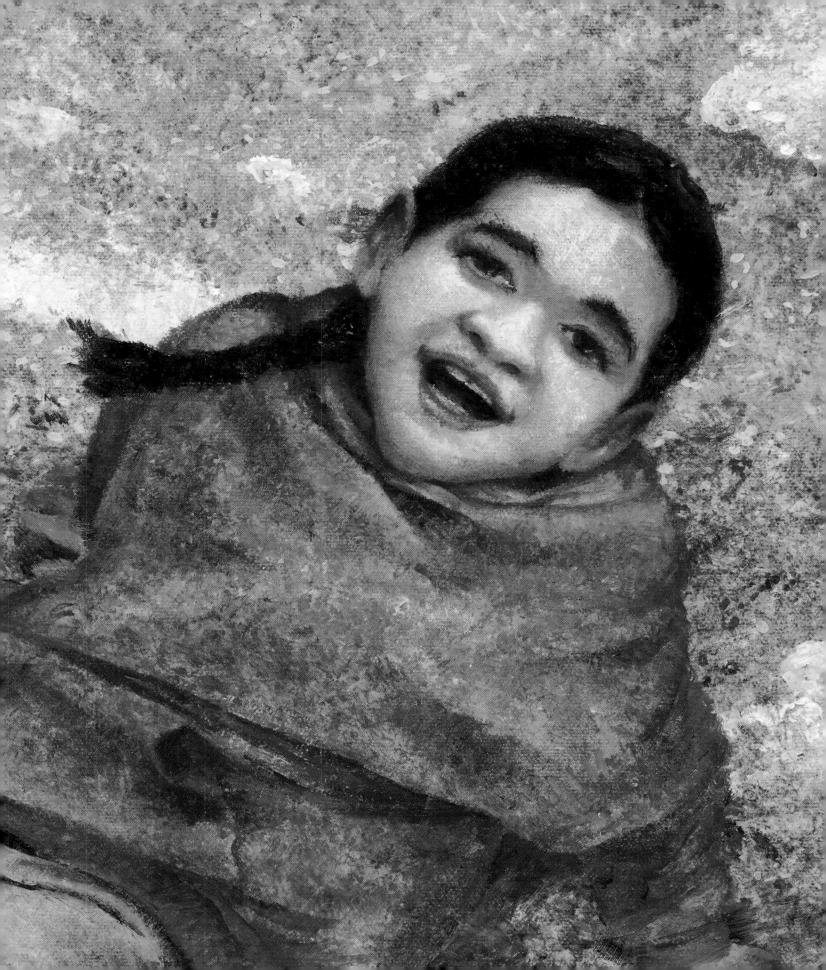

"atihk, atihk! ástam, ástam!" ká-nikamot Joe ékwa Cody kihtwám ká-nípawit
ékwa ká-nímihitot tápiskóc acihkosis. iyikohk sohki é-nímihitocik ékwa
é-nikamocik ékwa é-kitócikécik namwác ahpo é-péhtákik anima kíkway
ká-péhtákwaniyik.

"Ateek, ateek! Astum, astum!" Joe played and sang as Cody got up and danced like a young caribou. They were so busy dancing and singing and playing kitoochigan that they didn't hear the rumbling.

Mama and Papa were sitting near the fire, drinking tea.

"Thunder?" Mama asked Papa. "In May?"

"Can't be," said Papa. "Not until summer."

"Then what can it—" But Mama never finished her question.

mámá ékwa pápá kisiwahk kotawán é-kisákami-htihkécik.

"é-kitocik cí?" mámá ká-kakwécimát pápáwa.

"ékwa kéyápic é-síkwahk piko?"

"namwác étikwé," ká-itwét pápá. "namóya céskwa nípin, wacistakác!"

"kíkway máka..." namwác máka mámá ahpo kaski-htáw ka-kís-ayimiht.

hé, kéhtátawé mihcét atihkwak sisikoc ká-pimpahtácik.

nipahi mihcét atihkwak ká-pimpahtácik ékota mitoni táwáyihk kotawánihk ékwa
aniki níso nápésisak.

hé, é-nipahi-mihcéticik atihkwak.

Faster than lightning, a thousand caribou burst from the forest.
Two thousand caribou ran between the cooking fire and the boys.
Ten thousand caribou filled the meadow like a lake.

Joe stood in the middle of the plunging caribou. Through the tangle of their rushing legs and antlers, he could just see Cody, small as a doll, sitting on the caribou moss.

Joe took one step, then another, as if swimming through the snorting, steaming bodies, until he reached his brother.

ékota ká-nípawit Joe mitoni táwáyihk ita ká-pim-pahtácik atihkwak. ékota oskátiwáwa ékwa otéskaniwáwa ká-wápamát Codywa, é-apisísisiyit é-apiyit askíhk.

nisihkác ká-pimohtét Joe, tápiskóc atámihk nip-ihk é-pimátawít, isko ká-otihtawát osímisa.

ékwa ispihk ká-otinák Cody ocihciyiwa tápiskóc é-isi-nísicik
nisihkác é-pimihácik . kéhtátawé ékota ká-cípatapicik tahkóc
mistasiníhk, Cody é-tahkótapit Joe oskáta, kitócikan táwáyihk
aniki níso nápésisak. otéskanak piko ká-wápamácik. atihk osita
mína piko ká-péhtákwáw, okitówak tápiskóc é-itéyi htákosiniyit.

"atihk, atihk! ástam, ástam!" ká-nikamot ékwa kihtwám Joe,
"atihk, atihk! ástam, ástam!"

When he took Cody's hand they seemed to float right through the herd. The next thing they knew they were perched on the big rock, Cody on Joe's lap, kitoochigan between them. All they could see were antlers. And all they could hear were hooves, drumming all around them like thunder.

"Ateek, ateek! Astum, astum!"
Joe sang again. "Caribou, caribou!
Come, come!"

kéhtátawé ká-péhtákwáw kotak kíkway nápésisak, tápiskóc awiyak kímóc é-ayimiyit pihcáyihk
asiníhk ohci.

"Cody! Joe!" ká-itwét ana awiyak. "ástam, ástam!"
piyis ka-ohpinákwáw ospitoniwáwa nápésisak,
tápiskóc ta-nátácik awiya.

And out of the drumming came the voice of the herd,
whispering and moaning and wailing as it flowed past the rock.

"Cody! Joe!" it said. "Come, come!" And the boys
opened their arms to embrace the spirit.

When the river of caribou had become a trickle,
the brothers heard another wailing sound.
Mama's face was buried in Papa's parka.

"Woof, woof!" Ootsie danced around the great big rock.
"Ho-ho!" Papa sang out. But when Mama looked up at Papa's
face, she didn't see tears but a smile as bright as the sun.

ispihk atihkwak ékwa awasimé ká-péhtákosicik, kotak kíkwaya
ékwa mína ká-péhtákwáw nápésisak.
omámáwáwa ékota ká-nípawiyit tápiskóc é-káták wihkwákan
onápéma oskotákayihk.

"woof! woof!" Otisiy ká-papámi-kwáskohtit ékota kisiwahk
mistasiníhk.
"ho-ho!" ká-nikamot pápá. máka ispihk onápéma ká-kanawá-
památ mámá, namóya mátow pápá. pahpiw.

For there, atop the large rock, sat Joe and
Cody, laughing and laughing and laughing.

ayis ékota ká-cípatapicik tahkóc mistasiníhk
Joe ékwa Cody, é-pahpicik ékwa é-pahpicik,
ékwa é-pahpicik.

CARIBOU SONG

Text copyright © 2001 by Tomson Highway.
Illustrations copyright © 2001 by Brian Deines.
All rights reserved.
No part of this book may be used or reproduced
in any manner whatsoever without prior written permission
except in the case of brief quotations embodied in reviews.
For information address HarperCollins Publishers Ltd,
55 Avenue Road, Suite 2900,
Toronto, Ontario, Canada M5R 3L2.

http://www.harpercanada.com

HarperCollins books may be purchased for educational, business, or sales promotional use.
For information please write: Special Markets Department, HarperCollins Canada,
55 Avenue Road, Suite 2900, Toronto, Ontario, Canada M5R 3L2.

First edition

Canadian Cataloguing in Publication Data

Highway, Tomson, 1951–
Caribou song

Texts in English and Cree.
ISBN 0-00-225522-7

I. Deines, Brian II. Title.

PS8565.I433C37 2001   jC813'.54   C2001-901167-9
PZ7.H5444Ca 2001

01 02 03 04 05 DWF 7 6 5 4 3 2 1

Printed and bound in Canada